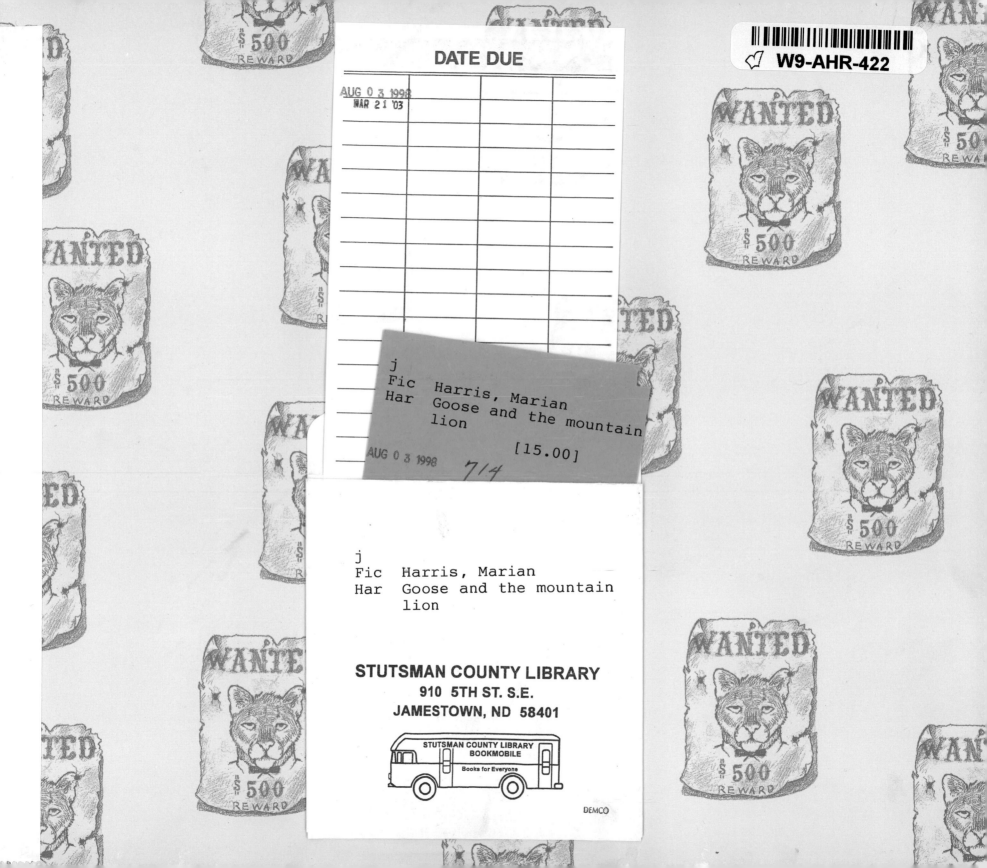

Northland Publishing

Goose
AND THE
Mountain
Lion

WRITTEN BY **Marian Harris** ILLUSTRATED BY **Jim Harris**

FIRST EDITION

ISBN 0-87358-576-3
Library of Congress Catalog Card Number 93-45424
Cataloging-in-Publication Data
Harris, Marian, 1961-
Goose and the mountain lion / written by Marian Harris ; illustrated by Jim Harris. — 1st ed.
p.   cm.
Summary: The other animals in the barn suspect a mountain lion of stealing
Goose's eggs, but when they stand guard, the eggs keep disappearing anyway.
ISBN 0-87358-576-3 : $14.95
[1. Geese—Fiction. 2. Pumas—Fiction.]
I. Harris, Jim, 1955-   ill. II. Title.
PZ7.H24225Go   1994
[E]—dc20   93-45424

Cover design by Trina Stahl
Designed by Trina Stahl and Rudy J. Ramos
Edited by Kathryn Wilder

Manufactured in Hong Kong by Wing King Tong

0470/7.5M/5-94

I HAVE A NEIGHBOR, Bill Clark, whose great-grandparents arrived in the Plateau Valley in Colorado—where I now live—in a covered wagon. Things were pretty rough back then, what with flooding in the springtime, droughts plaguing the summers, and blizzards and unbearable cold in the winter. But, to hear the old-timers tell it, it wasn't the wild weather in the middle of the Rocky Mountains that made them want to up and leave—it was the mountain lions that kept stealing their cows!

To save their livestock, the pioneer ranchers tried every guard animal they could think of—dogs, oxen, boars, billy goats—but nothing kept away the lions. Finally, Bill's great-grandparents put a goose in the corral, and, you guessed it, they learned that geese could, in fact, chase off a mountain lion!

Owning watch-geese is still a common practice in some parts of the West. Geese is plural for goose, which is also a word for the female of the species; a male goose is a gander. Most kinds of geese mate for life. A goose will sit on a nest with four to eight eggs in it, which hatch after twenty-six to twenty-seven days. When the baby geese, called goslings, appear, they latch on to the first thing they see. This is usually their mother, but sometimes it's a person, or even a pet, which they follow around dutifully.

Mountain lions, also called cougars and pumas, can weigh as much as a person—130 to 180 pounds—but can be up to eight feet long from the black tips of their tails to their fuzzy faces. The number of these lions, and the range in which they live, has gotten much smaller after years of lion hunting, trapping, and poisoning. Today they are listed as "threatened" and "endangered" in many states, which means there are so few of them that they are in danger of disappearing forever, but some people are working hard to protect them.

Pack rats, on the other hand, are in no danger of disappearing. These cute rodents make stick houses in trees or the corners of abandoned buildings, where they store any objects that catch their fancy, especially shiny things like coins and spoons. When angry or frightened, pack rats stomp their hind feet as loud as they can.

—M.H.

ONCE UPON A TIME, in an old barn made of cottonwood, there lived a goose. She was a fine goose, with a clutch of four creamy-white eggs just about ready to hatch.

One night, as the stars twinkled outside and the goose was almost asleep on her nest, she heard voices.

"It's been drinking at the creek," whispered the fuzzy-eared burro. "I saw its paw prints in the mud."

"It walked through the sagebrush, too," muttered the ox. "I saw its fur snagged on a twig."

"It came into the corral," added the brown and white goat. "I smelled its scent floating in the air."

"What is it?" cried Goose, leaping from her nest.

"It's a cat," answered the goat.

"A huge, hungry, yellow cat," shuddered the burro.

"It's a mountain lion!" thundered the ox.

Goose's stomach felt wobbly. She was afraid of cats. What if the mountain lion was hungry for goose? What if it smelled her in the old cottonwood barn? What if it came and ate her up?

Goose did not sleep well that night. She tossed and turned. She fussed and fidgeted. Once she dreamt she felt a mountain lion poking her in the belly. She opened one eye and looked around, but all she saw was a pack rat waddling quietly away to his home of mud and sticks outside the barn door.

Goose was relieved when she woke up the next morning and found that she hadn't been eaten by a big yellow cat. She stretched her wings and yawned. That's when she saw it—one of her eggs was missing! There were only three eggs left in her nest!

Big goose tears dripped on the straw. Drip, sniff; drip, sniff. Soon there was a puddle.

The goat poked his head over his stall door. "Oh my!" he exclaimed. "Is it a flash flood?"

"No!" sobbed Goose, dripping even more tears into the puddle. "It's much worse than that. Last night the mountain lion stole one of my precious eggs!"

"Foot rot!" sputtered the goat, stamping his black hooves. "That's what I'll get, standing in this puddle. I'll have to scare that mountain lion away, or I'll go lame, sure enough."

That night the goat stood guard outside the cottonwood barn. All night he watched for the mountain lion. He stopped watching only once — to pry a stone out of his hoof. Somehow, he never saw the mountain lion.

But when the sun shone into the cottonwood barn the next morning another egg had vanished. "Sssspit!" hissed Goose. "Sssspit! Sssspit!" Goose spit sprayed everywhere.

"What's this?" snorted the ox. "Have we sprung a leak?"

"Not a leak!" spit Goose. "A lion! Don't you see—the mountain lion has stolen another of my eggs. Sssspit! Sssspit, sssssssspit!"

"I do see," said the ox, "that if I'm ever going to be dry again, I'll have to stop that lion myself."

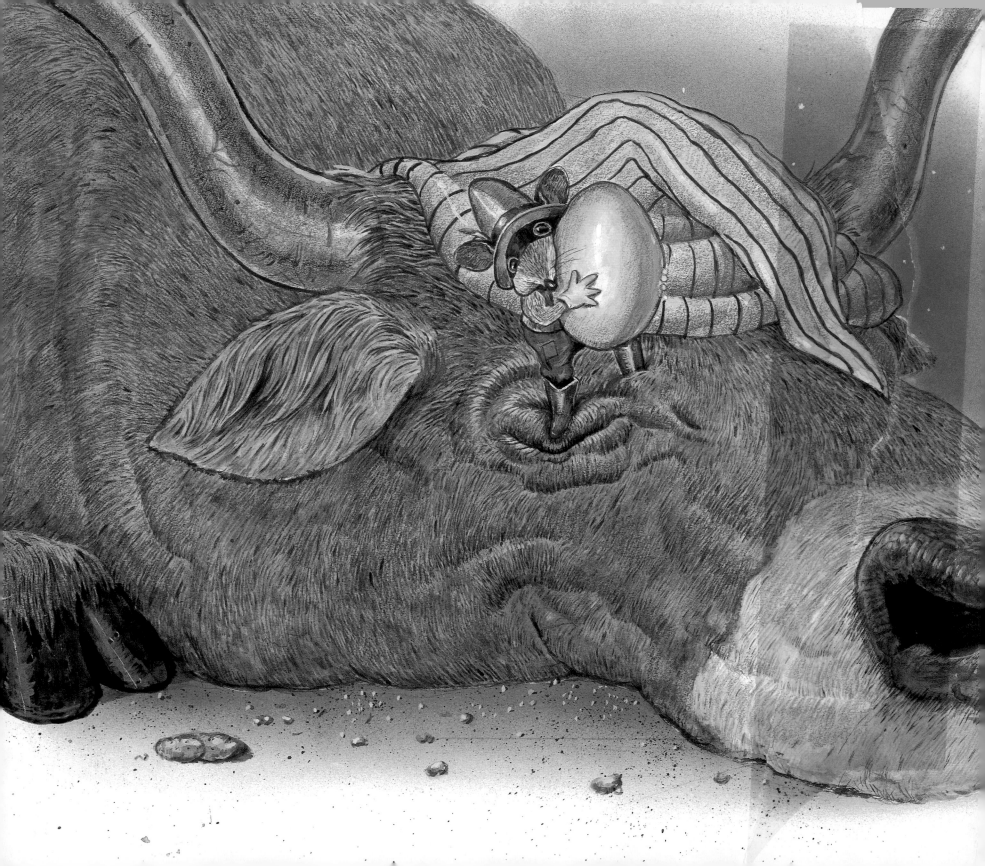

That night the ox stood guard, watching for the mountain lion. The ox was so huge he just turned sideways and blocked the whole barn door. Now, he thought, settling his chin into the dirt as he lay down for a nice dry snooze, no one at all can get those eggs, not even a mountain lion.

He was wrong. The next morning another egg was gone, and Goose flew into a rage. Around and around she flew; faster and faster she flapped her wings. A cloud of feathers filled the old cottonwood barn.

The burro, who was trying to eat her breakfast, suddenly found she had a mouthful of gray goose feathers. "Ptuui! Ptuui!" She stared hard into the swirling cloud. In the middle she saw Goose's nest, with only one egg left in it.

"If I don't keep that mountain lion away from that egg," muttered the burro, "I'll eat nothing but feathers as long as I live."

The burro was a very good guard. Most of the night she stood quietly staring into the sagebrush, searching the dark for the mountain lion. Sometimes she practiced how she would kick it away when it crept too close. This also helped shake the last few goose feathers from her nose. But the burro never saw the mountain lion. The only thing she came close to kicking was a pack rat, who happened to be passing that way.

The next morning, the burro was shocked to hear that Goose's nest was totally empty. Not an egg was left. Of course, she didn't go see for herself—it sounded like a hailstorm inside the old barn!

There were no eggs in Goose's nest that night.
There was no guard outside the barn door. But
there *was* a mountain lion.

It sniffed the air. It smelled a goose. Hmmm,
thought the mountain lion, I haven't had goose
in a long, long time. The big yellow cat crept
through the sagebrush and past the corral. It slid
through the door of the old cottonwood barn. Its
jaws opened wide for a bite of fresh juicy goose.

But there wasn't a goose in the barn. There was a monster. A hideous, howling monster. The monster whirled around and around and threw gray goose feathers in the mountain lion's eyes. The monster's feet slapped at the mountain lion's fur. Its orange bill snapped at the mountain lion's neck, and it hissed and honked in the lion's ears.

The burro, the goat, and the ox couldn't remember seeing such a hideous monster ever before.

The mountain lion decided it wasn't hungry for goose after all. "Eeeeeeeeeow!" it screamed, streaking out the barn door, past the pack rat mound, through the sagebrush, over the creek, and away beyond the darkened bluffs.

The ox, the goat, and the burro stared at the blackness inside the barn, trying to catch another glimpse of the hideous monster. But the monster had disappeared, too. All they saw now was . . .

One Mama Goose. Four baby geese.
And a very surprised pack rat.

MARIAN HARRIS has wanted farm animals since she was a child, but owning chickens or goats in a Chicago suburb would have pushed her family beyond the limits of neighborly tolerance. It wasn't until Marian had married and moved to a 200-acre farm in Indiana that she was able to have her dream. Sheep, goats, chickens, rabbits, and a pony inhabited the barns she remodeled, and later provided inspiration for stories. She now lives near Mesa, Colorado, with her husband, Jim; their children, Heather and Jimmy; Jim's brother, Paul; and a pair of Toulouse geese named Thanksgiving and Christmas.

JIM HARRIS has been illustrating for clients as diverse as the National Wildlife Federation and Sesame Street since 1983. His work has been recognized in *Who's Who in the Midwest*, in *Communication Arts*, and by the Society of Illustrators. In 1992, Jim teamed up with author Susan Lowell to make *The Three Little Javelinas* — a Reading Rainbow book — Northland's top-selling children's book ever. The Harris homestead sits at the end of a winding dirt road, where elk have been known to walk across the deck of Jim's studio, and where, however unwillingly, the female Toulouse goose modeled for *Goose and the Mountain Lion*.